NEXT IN LINE

NEXT IN LINE

POEMS

ANNETTE BARNES

PINYON PUBLISHING
Montrose, Colorado

Cover Art "Step Up" by Annette Barnes

Drawing of Annette Barnes by Basil Gogos

Design by Susan Entsminger

First Edition: August 2017

Pinyon Publishing
23847 V66 Trail, Montrose, CO 81403
www.pinyon-publishing.com

Library of Congress Control Number: 2017951245
ISBN: 978-1-936671-45-8

CONTENTS

I. SOME DEATHS

II. LET THE REST OF US SLEEP

I

SOME DEATHS

WHAT WE WANT

1.
In books I've read about that war a nurse's hand
could tell the cold of night from the cold of death,
which of the wounded could or could not wait.
Some of them tried not to cry, a few apologised
for dying and one, who lived in no man's land off
bottles of water he pulled from the dead, said:
    They got my fat but not my skin.

2.
A century later, this is London: they got the man
but not the fire he'd tried to put out. The underwear
shop's ablaze, six go homeless, a boy steals two bottles
of water, another trainers and televisions, some steal
from stealers and young girls boast, looting wine:
    We can do what we want.

3.
I'll have all, I say, pointing to the box of mushrooms
from the mainland. Then you'll have to pick them
yourself, says the clerk. They grow wild on the island.
    She means sharing's not optional.

4.
War, by other means, the looting. They wanted power,
said the woman, like animals on a short leash who
discover the leash is gone and suddenly take off,
    thinking freedom's free.

5.
The view from up here swarms with light the way
bees pulse a hive, but you must climb up before
you can hear the souls of the fallen rise.

LULL

The watch on his wrist tells time
he's run out of, shot at close range
playing football on Remembrance
Sunday, against a team whose side
of the war he thought he was on.

Green on blue deaths, they call
them; imagining yourself safe
when the wolf's wearing wool.

On Facebook a teenager posts
an obscenely captioned picture
of a burning poppy. Cheaply
made, they keep falling off.

The guns of Europe fell silent in 1918
on the eleventh hour of the eleventh day
of the eleventh month for not long enough.

THE UNDERGROUND

He leans on the bulwark next to her seat,
  his finger tips yellow against the glass,
she's close enough to read his palm,
  see whether he'll have a long life.

A man opposite excuses himself for
  sneezing. A man to her right reads
a Polish to English Dictionary, an Italian
  woman photographs her boyfriend.

At the last stop, a worker collects
  the trash that's been left. For months
after the bombings she took the bus
  but dying above ground is still dying.

REPAIR

The butcher barters beef for a cream to make
the elder of his two wives wrinkle free for a day

while the aging principessa who cannot face
the latest face the surgeon gives her takes

an overdose. I tolerate my imperfections but
ask the plasterers to fill the hairline cracks in

study walls. The mortician can do what he will.

WHOM DO YOU TRUST?

The faces
Arbus saw
scared her.
They scare
me too.

If he
won't look
you in the eyes
he may be lying.

If he stares at you,
he may be lying.

If he does
none of these,
he may be lying.

Even the dead
wear younger faces
in their coffins.

WITHOUT APOLOGY

Things happen. We've been promised
a meteor shower, though we can't see

a single shooting star. A man bumps into
us on the Underground without apology.

The fly we fish from our wine glass is
a recovering alcoholic, can't walk straight

but remembers how to fly. Peter remembers
how to fold his napkin, pour salt and pepper

on his food. We feel him feeling this world's
a fearful place. It happened when the hostel

was sold, backpackers littered the square,
talking loudly in foreign tongues, the police ran

complaints by the new night manager. Now
Peter stares at the tourists flooding the cathedral

and when we turn for a moment, he has fled.
And now a hand restrains him. What is it called,

salt shaker, person, weather? Why does hair
grow from his ears, why aren't his trousers clean?

Exactly. A world where beauty no longer counts.

FOUND WANTING

Unable to follow the words on the screen,
Brian weakly clapped his hands, smiling
faintly when he recognized his caregiver.

The conductor acts out the words for
patients to sing but Brian was lost, no
longer knows who he is, the only mercy.

When his older siblings finished playing
cowboys, Jojo got the gun and put
the muzzle in his mouth. It wasn't lethal

like the Lego piece—we made him spit
that out—but we recoiled. As we did when
the philosophy professor asked us to imagine

blow-torching an infant, lest we think nothing
was ever absolutely wrong.

Sometimes we're expected to recoil,
sometimes it's the worst thing we can do.

ONE TOO MANY

Anne lost her nerve at Beachy Head. She could not leap (tomb-
stoning they call it) or walk, her pockets filled with stones, into

the sea. Come stay with me, she asks of her sisters. But lives
are always lived elsewhere, so in a wood outside Oxford she finds

a tree on which to hang. Her children grieve. In the church where
visitors disregard the suggested donation we light candles for the

usual reasons. After my father died, mother would say, I want to die,
but she always took her medications. My brother said, I haven't

slept in days, before he fell asleep in his warm bath and I began
to measure lives in black plastic bags I filled with the remainders.

One day I say, I am tired of cleaning up after the dead so my husband
promises not to die before me. He's always been good that way.

CLOSING TIME

1.
How are you feeling?
Bad, which is good, he said,
so she knew he was ready.

Are you still ill?
Emphysema, he said impatiently.
She'd meant the bronchitis.

House-bound, he called it Ward
78, struggled to breathe,
passed the phone to his partner.

He'd joke about falling off the perch.
Now he was angry doctors wouldn't
overdose him, but the morphine

calmed him down. He wanted to die
in his sleep in his own bed and did.

2.
Imagine changing politics only when
changing lovers, who get younger
and more conservative with each decade.

Speaking softly without being soft, crossing
borders—race, gender, age—but keeping
the bonds to wife and three grown children.

Laughing—and oh how he could—
at the world, if not always at yourself.

GOING, GOING, GONE

I think you can guess
why I'm calling,
Brian's partner said.
When? I asked.
Yesterday. Peacefully
in his sleep.

Peter, John, Brian,
but only John knew
who he was
when he died.

SOME DEATHS AT BARKSTON GARDENS

1.
We could see Henrietta's window from ours.
Her shade went up earlier. And down earlier too.

We hung rice on her door when her oncologist
suggested it would help with the chemotherapy.

Phillida drove her to appointments, Mary and Jose
brought violets, but she moved beyond our help.

2.
After his son Waldo died, Emerson said grief
was teaching him how shallow it was. Now she

cannot turn the pages of her books, the cancer
eating through her the way the rat in the novel

eats through seabirds straying aboard the ship,
their bones breaking like crystal.

3.
I kill slugs with paper towels, not salt, watch
night fall on the blackbird under the plane tree.

I let pregnant women and old men have my seat
on buses and trains, give buskers bits of change,

haul wearable clothes off to Oxfam. If God's
in the details, might these small mercies count?

4.
When love was requited by chance, one petal
a wish—He loves me—one petal a fear—He

loves me not—we thought we had outsmarted
fate. The viburnum and its fungus are at war

now and it could go either way. In retrospect
we'd ask a different question.

MEMENTO MORI

Her mother's ashes were
lighter than her brother's,
or maybe it was just the box.

She wants to dress richly in
her coffin in the going out
gown she bought at auction.
No more black tie dinners.

When Caesar drops down
next to her unprotected front
row seat, struck by righteous
conspirators, death leans in again.

At the farmers market an angel
in a bicycle basket wishes the
butcher *Bonne Année*; he's back
from fighting another of our wars.

Wearing her wings over her winter
coat, she's too young to be in heaven
where only the dead are welcome.

WASTED

May morning, and the flowers of the Christmas
cactus open, fuchsia, for girls who like their
pleasures neon. She's been saying goodbye now
for several years but today feels like the last; he's
not just thin he's wasted, whatever he eats, what's
eating him eats more. A plant's gone missing that
weighs more than he does, urban poachers, they must
have had a time of it. But here's one coming back
from the dead with a few new leaves. She thinks
Miracle-Gro might help. Grief's a luxury for living.

A BRIEF ENCOUNTER

The bee flew in
while I was exercising.

Barely alive, it clung
to the edge of the paper
I shook out on the balcony.

I tried turning it wing side
up but it fell over.

It would have been more
merciful to step on it,
a friend said, but I suspect
dying whole is better.

COLLATERAL DAMAGE

She promised the hermit crab
she'd take it back to the beach
but by morning it was dead.

She hadn't, as shell books
recommend, boiled a live creature
to get its shell, she thought the
shell empty, but she had turned

a house into a coffin, its burial
at sea, not a homecoming.

THE TANAGER

The car that hits it does not
stop but we do. The vet says

it can't live long and, for
a small fee, ensures it doesn't.

It weighed so little, its scarlet
feathers too light for the May frost.

MINDFUL

for GAC

He told jokes to keep his young son awake
on the way to the hospital. In a favourite,
a philosopher and economist, furious with
the golfers ahead of them for playing slowly,
learn that they're blind. He'd laugh when he'd
tell it, his shoulders bouncing up and down.

He did not find inequality funny, wanted
us to see the arguments for it could never
be any good. He felt blessed although he
did not believe anyone had blessed him.

The manciple found him in his study.
No chance of recovery, the doctor said.

We said goodbye in a chapel not used to Hebrew
prayer, or, for that matter, to Irving Berlin.

The memorial was elsewhere, in a beautiful
library, built by a man who earned his money
growing sugar in a place that was safely far away.
And all of us, the white, the black, the hundreds
in our many voices, sang the hymn our friend had
favoured most of all: Solidarity Forever, a good
old union song. In the joke, the philosopher's
remorseful, the economist recommends night play.

NO END IN SIGHT

I used to light a candle for D,
the first of my friends to die.
One serves many now. Make
a wish, my mother would say,
but don't tell anyone what it is.

At the far end of the cathedral
the Holy Trinity in Glory looks
down on me. It's not right to win
at your own party, she said,
when I blew the candles out.

UNEXPECTEDLY

After the meal, a caterwaul,
perhaps of pride,
though the prey in his bowl
came from a can.

Some times when we play
catch the ribbon
he tires before I do. We first met

in the passage way
between the house he lived in
and the house I did.

Like his Burmese ancestors,
who, they say, would ride
into battle, he jumps on my shoulder,
purrs in my ear. I've never told him
I'd once been allergic to cats.

When an unexpected fall
puts his owner in hospital,
I'm a surrogate feeder.
He's the lucky one. Decades ago,

at midnight my lawyer called,
his mood merrier than official.
What if the cat predeceases you?
he asked, a likelihood I'd not
anticipated. Herding Cats,

like apologising when you know
you're right, is unseemly and possible
only if you think the alternative's worse.
It sometimes is. But not yet.

IF IT'S NEEDED

An umbrella just in case it rains,
an understudy just in case of illness,

are less troubling precautions than
the just in case shoebill its mother

allows her healthy first born to peck
when food is scarce. It's rarer for

Homo Sapiens to think a child's a spare.
The man on the pavement mutters

spare change at passers by as if
they carried money just in case.

SPENCER HILL

is steep, so breathing hard we sink down into a front pew,
while the pallbearers, in the rich black of 16th century

prosperity, step down into the sanctuary, easily balancing
her wooden coffin, whom we knew only in these last years,

whom we recognize but do not remember as the girl whose hair
flowed down to her waist and whose skirts reached her ankles.

A poet's voice, the tape is old, telling us how we should think
about death, and we rise into the air sweetened by multitudes

of lilies and the choir's evensong. At the reception, the prawn
and cucumber sandwiches remind us to be grateful and I confess

to the priest I no longer go to church. Why don't you come to
Midnight Mass? he says. I can only think of tears. For whom?

For Marjorie? For you whose ashes arrived in the post for whom
we did not sing? I saw how small the coffin was that held her.

BRIGHTON

Early for your memorial party we sit
windblown on a bench by the lifeguard
under his umbrella, yellow as a crayon,
following a lone swimmer, seagulls adrift,

the beach mostly stones. They're planning
a hedge for you in the communal garden
where you always served us white wine.
Would you have wanted a tree instead?

It came in the mail on Monday, the picture
you sent from Norway, wearing that funny
Viking helmet, grinning at the camera.
and that note on the back—Even if this

trip kills me, I won't mind. You would
have minded a friend falling after toasting
you. Down he went, fracturing his skull, his
hip, I don't know what more the x-rays

showed. But in the evening the sun
shining on moist air gave us a rainbow.

SHE MADE IT HERS

The night my father died
my mother screamed,
and woke the neighbours,
and that was just the start.

I'd come home from school
and find her curled up in
a corner of the bedroom,
indifferent to everything
but her own grief.

WHAT THE DEAD CANNOT DO

My brother is dead she told them
when she paid his final telephone bill

but the man called back, wanting
further payment. He's dead, she said

but he persisted. Are you sure he
didn't make those calls? Ashes in

a box under ground have limited
powers, she said, but she could tell

he only half believed her. They
don't always get the causes right.

He drowned because he fell asleep
in the bath because he was over tired

because he was overworked because,
but that he was dead, they got that right.

THE ONLY TIME
SHE LIVES ALONE

Just as the dog knows
he's being surveyed
by the hawks whose
claws are out, she
knows the man who
killed the woman
living below her
tried her door first.

Knows too choosing
an executioner is
problematic,
neither wanting, nor

not wanting, the right
motivation. When
asked what kind

of man was needed
to do his job, a former
hangman answered:
a sensitive man.

DONE FOR

Here We Go
Lyttelton Theatre, 2015

A nurse
slips
clothes off
and on
an old man
in seamless
iterations,

They move
together
in silence.

The nights
and days
that come
between
dressing and
undressing
are left out,
as if they
didn't count.

FERTILIZER

It depends on how far down you
go before you find the bone.

In bulk from battlefields:
Leipzig, Austerlitz, Waterloo,

used like the salt and soot,
the woollen rags and hooves,

to improve London's soil.
Napoleonic warriors lie deep.

Sometimes, closer to the surface
the pulverised parts of slaughtered

animals: the blood meal, bone meal,
hides, hoofs and horns.

Soil's not sold in garden shops
in England. You don't want people

digging up the earth, the clerk said,
when I asked for some.

II

LET THE REST OF US SLEEP

AT THE POST OFFICE

I'm in line at my branch to post a gift I haven't
quite described on the customs declaration for

a friend across the sea who also spends time
mailing things to me, but says it could be worse:

'in Bucharest one waits for hours, only to have
the window crash down an inch from your

fingers—"smoking break" says the sign,' or
so he thinks. Well, not only is there a long

wait here, the man in front of me and the man
behind me are shouting at a woman who's

packed three boxes of books, which the clerk
suggests she pack as one so she's untying the

string now, while time slows. Three clerks where
there used to be nine and the woman's shouting

back now. I'm not sure what angers them more:
because she's hesitating or because she's foreign.

The man behind me, foreign too, manages abusive
English nicely. Anyway, if my gift fails to arrive,

the receipt proving it was posted may track it down.
I hope you'll be pleasantly surprised. I'm next in line.

WOMEN DRESSING AND UNDRESSING

When my mother, trying to shame me into eating,
told me about children starving in India, I spaghetti
tied the brown balls on my plate to send to them, but

she sent me to bed instead. So when the woman at
the mirror asks me how she looks in the one size fits
all jumpers, I don't remind her of the starving. Shame's
the problem in the first place. I say, that doesn't suit
you. I do not say, nothing will unless you lose six stone.

The master painters, who liked their women fleshy, knew
to paint them nude or fully clothed, not in their underwear.

Too few mirrors, a woman had said, and we all in the common
changing room had a similar thought. But we were patient,
waited our turn to look, unaware, perhaps, that shame's the cure.

MENAGERIE

The blond woman's leg wound oozes, her
friend towels up the spill, a young man

coughs but covers his mouth. The daughter
of the old man in the wheel chair is anxious,

but the young African girl acts as if she's
on a family holiday. He's wearing a rugby

shirt, the Englishman whose arm's in
a sling, a woman has bandaged fingers.

A red faced newborn howls, the well dressed
French couple read the Sunday paper, two

young Chinese stand, all seats taken. When
the woman next to me notices my arm in its cast,

she asks, Are you queuing for the disabled toilet?
No, I don't think of myself as disabled.

A broken wrist, more accident than emergency,
but still I haven't wasted anyone's time.

WIESENLAND

Pina Bausch's Tanztheater Wuppertal
London, July 2012

1.
We are not sure why women smoking while a man
pours water from one bucket to another & sometimes

wets their hair is particularly appropriate to Hungarian
pastureland, but it is as full of wonder as the scene of

men blowing smoke into a woman's hair, who is trailed
by a smoke cloud as she moves. Virtual pastureland hangs

at the back of the stage, which is brought forward and down
in the second half, a new space for the dancers to move in.

2.
A man lies on the grass. A woman comes by so he gets up,
brushes the ground for her to sit, then lies down elsewhere,

which motions repeat, the fulcrum of Pina's way with dance.
The whole company throws bags of bread to the audience,

which we presume is their way of inviting us to join them
for dinner on stage, where they sit around a table pretending

to eat with delicious dance-like moves. The standing ovation
lasts and lasts, the dancers' eyes filling with tears.

3.
A young man sitting too far back wanted to know whether the dancers had asked people in the front row if they loved someone. We said we'd been asked and answered we did. And probably we meant it.

AT THE DUANE HANSON EXHIBITION

Serpentine Galley
London, 2015

They're all ordinary people—the black man
spattered with the pink he's been roller painting

on a wall, the black woman with a cart of fluids,
about to clean another room, the cowboy standing

against a wall, the overweight farmer on a John Deer
tractor, the plump white woman selling old books

and bad paintings—but their telling-you-nothing faces
in their life-like bodies troubles you. But it's only when

you see the bin crammed with trash, the crushed cans,
splintered umbrella, empty box of All, and the dead

grey baby, its head still in the plastic bag, that you
really feel threatened. No one poses for selfies with it.

IF SHAKESPEARE

The Merchant of Venice
London, 2015

The woman sitting next to me has a cold,
The woman sitting next to her is old.

They seem to be grand-parent related.
Although the likeness in the old one looks deflated.

The younger one likes the play,
the other one does not say.

They both are Jews, may I presume?
or, for the sake of the poem, assume?

If Shakespeare were to be reconceived by a mind
that in a Las Vegas casino one might find,

the anti-Semitism might be as blatant,
the homosexuality as latent.

Portia might be a game show prize
and Elvis-like feelings of the right size.

Tragedy would be no more,
mockery would have the floor.

The younger could think such outright display
was surely to be seen in the showing-up way,

so many are the pathways of disgrace
one could understand the old woman's face.

IMPERFECTIONS OF
EVERYDAY LIFE

A small grey bearded dog, with
a bandy hind leg, trots lopsidedly,
undiminished, hungry
for the world,
which he knows chiefly
through his nose,
his quarrel with the leash.

Boys in red caps and jackets kick
a soccer ball, tread on the daffodils.

The women to her left talk right
through the mid-week matinee,
take no notice of attempts
to quiet them.

A man at dinner wanders into
territory he imagines to be
philosophy, certain that no one
can be certain about anything.

Living on a planet whose core of
molten rock erupts infrequently
allows us to be careless.

MONEY MATTERS

Nivolumab, Kadcyla
Star War warriors or

cancer drugs too
costly for the NHS?

It isn't as if money
is just for luxuries.

KNOWING HOW

To reward behaviour you want
try chicken till the cat sits where

you tell it to long after you leave,
because the vase falls. The child

says the cat did it. You punish him
so he becomes a better liar. The cat

jumps on the stove. You turn burners
on till the cat avoids the stove: best to

punish if the only way out is behaviour
you want. The cat feels free when it

chooses its spot, but not when it avoids
the stove. And remember you can't reward

a greedy cat if it's not hungry, nor a child
with money it does not know how to spend.

THE CAT

when annoyed,
wags her tail
like a spinster's finger,

is a Lady Macbeth
about cleanliness,

a Julia Child
about food.
Spends a night
licking Brie.

Learns only
what she wants:

a Houdini at
escape, opens
doors by their handles,

doesn't learn
to fetch.

Carries her weapons
concealed.

THE SQUIRREL

1.
Squeezing himself in,
 he over eats,
firemen bend the bars
 of the bird feeder
to free him.

2.
In the park a young girl
 cradles him in her arms,
others hold out peanuts.
 Holbein allows us to think
he once was a pet.

3.
In the plane tree he dismantles
 a rival's nest, flings its leaves
to the ground.

4.
Spends all afternoon
 burying chestnuts
left on the garden table.

5.
The farmer gives her
 the apples he can't sell.
She gives them to the squirrel.
 When the farmer learns this,
he stops giving her apples.

6.
Chewing through the power cable
 he shoots, like a lightning bolt,
into the garden, dead on arrival
 as the lights go out.

7.
Lavinia, who, on her
 eightieth birthday,
shot a hole in the ceiling
 with her new gun,
shoots him but never a bird.

LE MASCHERE E AI COSTUMISTI

When procreation's not the aim
who cares if the peacocks at
il Carnevale di Venezia aren't
displaying their own feathers.

Posing for the photographers
these carnival birds gloriously
strut, their merely human
imperfections hidden beneath
layers of velvet, silk and satin.

Delete the pictures I tell my
friend, the gown—a Dior!—
demands a face less
riddled by time and she,
as good friends do, assures
me the lighting was bad.

METERED LIGHT

1.
Once, when we'd run out
of coins, the warden left
the light on for two hours.

At noon when it closes,
candles for the dead blown
out, Mary and the child
looked at no more, is this
when he comes?

2.
Just Jesus nailed to his cross,
the thieves tied to theirs, one
nail to bind feet that must be
kept together. The drink he's
offered, more sour than thirst.

3.
On the road to Calvary, burdened
by his cross, Jesus falls. The patron
saint of photographers & laundry
workers catches his face on her veil.

The young girl watching
Christ crowned with thorns
has pulled up her skirt, is
about to lose her innocence.

4.
At Christ's first fall
the dog shows pity.

5.
Mindful of the fallen, the church asks
for donations for Haiti, some one pencils
in 'and Chile.' After Lisbon Voltaire said
God had some explaining to do.

RELIGION

Because I lived at three three three
the Trinity appealed to me.

Jesus crucified, a perfidy
that Judas made reality,

the Virgin birth, anomaly,
the Resurrection, mystery,

three, distinct in unity,
what more ask of Divinity.

PARIS: SNAPSHOTS

1. Luxembourg Gardens

The new turtle
spouting water
at the horses
in the fountain
is too green.

2. Musée d'Orsay

Painting nudes
from behind
Degas has caught
one scratching
her back.

3. Musée Carnavalet

In Atget's Paris,
the peddler, laden
with lampshades,
wears a hat.

4. Café Josephine

The foie gras
cannot be
resisted.

THE LOUVRE

A short introduction
to the Italian Renaissance

but only one young boy
looks at the paintings,

scribbles down
Domenico Ghirlandaio

Madonna and Child
before running to catch up;

his classmates are taking
photos for their Facebook friends.

BLACKBIRDING

He had to have it, Captain Cook,
the black bird that alighted on
the bowsprit of his ship. A benign
taking, as takings go. Turned out
to be a Caledonian crow.

Turns out this crow is very good
with tools. He makes a barb to reach
the grub that burrows beneath
the bark. Ingenuity in the hunt.

And pleasure in the ingenuity. How else
explain the likeness? Hunting in this case
creatures like us, whose bodies' shadows
on the wall darken during long sunsets.

Sing a song of slavery, a pocket full
of woe, from New Caledonia's harbor
to Queensland's sugar plantations.

BOY WITH FROG

Outside the Punta della Dogana beneath the statue of
Fortune which tells which direction the wind is blowing,
he's guarded against vandals by day, encased in plastic
at night. Slightly larger than life, eyes closed, oblivious
to the couples who stop to pose with him, dangling the frog
by one leg, he's naked, almost innocent. They were naked

too, the boys they moved as cargo here, on their way to places
they didn't want to go. The one with the frog's a duplicate.
His brother's an ocean away, on the steps of an American
museum. They're twins, same artist, same surface whiteness.
You can't tell them apart. Except for the rail they seem to
think they need there to keep the photographers at bay.

CAPE COD

1. Creatures don't come if I call

Laughing gulls bring spring, black ducks bring fall.

On the prow a woman next to me holds out her
hand,
  and in Lakota, the language of her Sioux father,
calls softly
  to the whales, humpbacks surfacing and diving
before us.

Why are you holding out your hand? she asks.
  I don't know, I say. Why do you ask?
I wanted to know how much you knew.

Once a whale leapt up to touch her face.
  Even she was surprised.

2. Creatures I don't call come

Seagulls hover;
a grey seal nibbles at a flounder
  till it fits its mouth.
We do not tell the fisherman
  the large black bird he thinks an osprey
is a buzzard. After winter's thaw
  more gather,
tell where corpses lie.

Gulls drop clam shells until they open.
  We once knew
how to do without a knife.

3. What one thing is to another

White pines replace the insect riddled trees
planted on farmland that felled a forest.
Phragmites are to cattails what farmland
is to forest, marsh crabs to beach grass,
whimbrels to hermit crabs.

That death's a part of life isn't a comfort.
Wind ruffling the kingfisher's feathers is.

4. What we seek

Clam diggers, competitors of moon
snails and gulls, arrive at low tide,
armed with shovels and sledges.

The seagull who follows as I look for
shells finds morsels, a seal snatches
the sea bass from the fisherman's line.
He'll eat better than me tonight, he says but
later catches another fish.

5. What turns

A kited water skier sails in two directions
 though the wind goes in one.
Squadrons of blue jays filling
 the pines fall silent.
The sea the storm turned brown turns blue.

ISTANBUL

1.
Let the rest of us sleep, the predawn call
for prayer is for the obstinate believer, who
at midday closes his shop and, shoeless,
in a space woven for him in a carpet, prays.

It was an old man, not him, we saw cursing
at the mosque door when, late to prayer, he
saw the pair of leopard skin pumps.

2.
At breakfast in the hotel gardens cats snatch
at the food we give them, scavengers or demi-
mondes, wary, only mildly tamed by tolerance.

In the wall sized photographs of ancient libraries
we see shelves upon shelves of books that are
admired but no longer read. The photographs,
like the books in them, are exquisite and costly.

Portraits of Ataturk line roads dense with cars;
a lift carved into the hillside takes us to fresher
air, replete with art, tea and chocolate cake.

Rich men, we learned as children, may put a bullet
through their head, kingdoms become colossal
wrecks, but look how much there is to want.

3.
Crows and bats float nightly round lit minarets,
the city's holy ghosts, but not yet its prophets.

CAPABILITY BROWN
GETS RICH

Opening up vistas
for the landed Gentry.

Seeding lawns.
Planting trees.

Good investments,
forests: the Empire

thirsty for wood
to build its ships.

Provide pleasure too:
hunting woodland

creatures the new guns
allow amateurs to kill.

Enough variety if seen on
horseback or in a coach.

Not meant for walking
as cows and peasants do.

At a distance, though,
the Ha-ha sees to that.

FIRE SAFETY

1.
At the awards ceremony
for the best essay on Fire
Safety in the Home I ask
my mother: which side
of the stage shall I go up
if I win? You won't win,
she says, but when I do
I go up the wrong side.

2.
My father asks: Do you
want a ham sandwich? I
say NO! & slam the door.

I burn everything I write
about him that was unkind.
The dead need no reminders.

3.
Memory, like damp,
darkens the photographs
of us looking happy.

4.
'NO', isn't a good last word.

QUICK LEARNER

When she was seven,
she used her allowance

to buy a lottery ticket.
A relatively easy way,

her father thought, for
her to learn about losing.

THE UNFORGIVEN

She roasted more
  than turkey
that Thanksgiving,
  the first after
her father died.

The money hidden
  in the oven
turned to ashes.

It didn't matter
  to her mother
that she hadn't known.

She cut herself
  to place the pain
where she could watch it.

DOING WELL

The Aston Martin
goes too fast
hits wet leaves.

She lies in a ditch,
the driver phones
for a mechanic
before he calls a doctor.

In hospital a young
boy tells her to keep
your pecker up,
the doctor speaks
of men landing
on the moon

but morphine's what
she needs.

She hoards
sleeping pills too

but it takes her
only a year
to learn
how to walk again.

YET

Her suitcase is packed.
She wants to go home.

Irritability, agitation,
the classic signs

of injury to the brain,
hers yet not hers.

It's the memories lost
not the fractured skull

or blood spilt that pains
the friends she asks to

help her escape. Guarded
around the clock by carers,

she has no privacy either,
herself yet not herself.

Her body's the same,
maybe even her soul.

I'm fine, she insists, but
the she she was is not.

DOWN AND OUT

On the concrete,
outside Waitrose.
Sometimes with
a dog.
Doesn't
in so many words
but.

TACT

Hairdressers are encouraged to talk about
food and vacations, but not sex, religion
and politics, so when Mark, who turns
silver strands to gold, is asked, Will you
vote Labour or Tory? he says, Undecided.

WHAT'S IT LIKE

'while crows play catch with themselves, i.e. flying up with a stick
they will then drop from a good height so they can dive down and
catch it before it grounds, ravens drop sticks for their mates to catch,
and vice versa, which crows never do …'

What's it like being among the first women
to teach at an all-male college? someone asks,
perhaps expecting her to be a raven, not a crow.
Newly married, learning to cook, she doesn't drop

sticks for other women to catch. When the dean,
his arm around her shoulder, says, I'm so glad you're
integrating, she smiles, as she does at graduation when
under her robe she wears a mini skirt and high boots.

Do you mind being viewed sexually? students ask
but when she tells them she doesn't view them
that way, they stop asking.

WHAT DOES IT TAKE TO
SPEAK THE SAME LANGUAGE?

Have a child,
a pregnant friend urges,
wanting us to understand each other,
but I don't.
Don't have a child?
Don't want us to understand each other?
Don't understand her wanting me
to have a child in order for us
to understand each other?

So many things to mean
it's a wonder
we ever understand one another.
Or just think we do.

TOPICS FOR A BOOK CLUB DISCUSSION

Recommended for ages six and above.

1. Sing a Song Of Six Pence

Is it right to bake blackbirds?
Do kings deserve a dish daintier
than cottage or shepherd's pie?

Consider whether being English
influences your answers. Would
a Chinese or an African answer in
the same way? Would a Scot?

2. Little Miss Muffet

Is a tuffet?
a. a clump of grass
b. a small hillock
c. a foot stool
d. a pillow
e. all of the above
f. none of the above

Should a spider have asked permission
to sit next to Miss Muffet?

Consider whether spiders can be held
to the same standard as humans.

3. Old King Cole

Was King Cole?
a. magnificent
b. old
c. a saint
d. planning to play the flute
f. eat some soup
g. being inconsiderate calling for things so late at night

Were any of the fiddlers women? Discuss whether their presence or absence should be of concern.

4. Humpty Dumpty

Was Humpty Dumpty
a. a King
b. a cannon
c. an egg

Did Humpty Dumpty merit the attention of so many of the King's men?

Discuss how one should allocate emergency relief resources.

LOOKED OUT MY WINDOW

On a grey morning,
preening, oiling
and aligning feathers,
water proofing and
readying for flight,

then the alert stillness
and silence,
head turning slowly,

framed
between the
branches and twigs.

Said to be
smart,
but can't imagine
what's it like to be a crow
on a grey morning
before it dives
down onto grass.

BOUGHT FISH

It's full of roe
the fishmonger says
and I ask him to keep it.

I'll eat the mother
and her future too.

BETTER LATE THAN NEVER

Yesterday I forgot to grind the pine nuts
with the basil, but did my best to fix it.
I mixed the whole ones in
& left the grinding to our teeth.

Today the chipper is whining while abseilers
go about their work in our plane tree. Skilful
with ropes they chain saw seven years' growth
of limbs. The postman stops to watch.

Men feed the shredder:
extracting fallen branches from the bushes
with long poles,
collecting those on the ground,
sweeping up the seed residue.

No nests are left, no cover
until the new leaves form.
Wood pigeons & crows will be disappointed,
but the robins and blackbirds are accustomed
to the lower shrubs.
They should pollard earlier, before the tree
behaves as if it were spring.

COMMUNAL GARDEN

In the afternoon
a foam-filled stars and stripes

softens the falls of the children
rushing to mount the mechanical bull.

The birthday party's American,
the garden square's English,
the exclamations of delight multi-lingual.

The fathers arrive at six,
violate the NO BALL GAMES sign.

Money men, rich enough
to buy into the square

and not obey
other people's rules.

THROUGH THE
CENTURIES

He kept a menagerie,
leopards, jackals,
hedgehogs, bulls,
bison and eagles,
future subjects
to be dissected.

Bribed men
for the corpse
of the Irish giant
who'd asked
to be buried
at sea.

When the
Underground
came, the great
house, by then
an asylum
for ladies
of limited lunacy
but sufficient means
was demolished.

Mansion blocks
were built, the
grounds reduced,
the space democratised
or so it seemed
until prices rose
and only the rich
could live in them.

Urban foxes disobey
the communal garden
sign forbidding them.
Rats do too. A gun's
thrown in, for a few
hours Calais refugees
housed in a nearby
hotel are allowed in,
but mostly it's children
and their nannies.

AUTUMN

In bramble bushes,
the withered blackberries

feed the bullfinches
that keepers of orchards

may no longer kill,
scarcity their new protection.

Partial to the cotoneaster berries,
the blackbirds and winter migrants quarrel.

THE HOURS BETWEEN

Ants in the peonies,
beetles in the lettuce,

between midnight &
three you're alone

unless someone's
breathing next to you.

ELSEWHERE

A middle of the afternoon darkness, clouds move
in slowly, birds take flight, the viburnum bends
as the wind increases. Then sheets of rain against
the glass, lightning, thunder, sirens. The clouds
lighten, the sky turns blue. A blackbird sips rain
water from the hydrangea's saucer, chirping
between sips. Elsewhere lovers pant between
kisses, butterflies sip tortoise tears and runners
reach finish lines. No bombs go off, no one dies.

ACKNOWLEDGMENTS

My thanks to the editors of the journals in which the following poems first appeared, some in slightly different forms.

Great River Review: "What We Want"
Lalitamba: "Topics for a Book Club Discussion
Plume: "Without Apology," "Spencer Hill"
Stand: "Some Deaths at Barkston Gardens," "Repairs," "A Mercy," "Blackbirding," "Cape Cod, "Whom Do You Trust?"
Hampden-Sydney Poetry Review: "As If" (an earlier version of "One Too Many")
Voyages: "At The Post Office," "Women Dressing And Undressing"

CPSIA information can be obtained
at www.ICGtesting.com
Printed in the USA
FSOW01n0037300817
38017FS